William Shakespeare

Dorothy Turner

Illustrations by Richard Hook

Great Lives

Available in paperback:

Beethoven
Henry VIII
Mary Queen of Scots
Queen Elizabeth I
Queen Victoria
William Shakespeare

First published in 1985 by
Wayland (Publishers) Limited
61 Western Road, Hove
East Sussex BN3 1JD, England

British Library Cataloguing-in-Publication Data

A catalogue record for this book is available
from the British Library.

HARDBACK ISBN 0-85078-495-6

PAPERBACK ISBN 0-7502-1329-9

Phototypeset by Kalligraphics Ltd, Redhill, Surrey
Printed and bound in Italy by G. Canale & C.S.p.A., Turin

Contents

Who was Shakespeare?

William Shakespeare was one of the greatest writers who ever lived. His plays have been translated into many languages and are constantly performed in countries all over the world, on stage and in films.

What was Shakespeare himself like? The simplest answer is that we do not know much about his life.

If he had lived in modern times we would have all kinds of information to help us know about him. Books, photographs and films would tell us much about his thoughts, his appearance and even the exact sound of his voice.

But Shakespeare lived in Tudor England four hundred years ago, in the time of Queen Elizabeth I.

We have much less information about people who lived in those days – we do not even know the full details of Queen Elizabeth's life. Shakespeare seems to have lived rather quietly, without attracting much attention to himself during his lifetime. But it is possible, by piecing together the little evidence we have about him, to build up an idea of how he led his life.

Shakespeare's family

William Shakespeare was born in April 1564, in Stratford-upon-Avon, in the heart of England. He was baptized in Stratford church on 26 April. We do not know the exact date of his birth but it is celebrated on 23 April – the same date as his death, fifty-two years later.

William's father, John Shakespeare, was a local farmer's son. He had moved into Stratford and set up business as a glove maker. William's mother, Mary Arden, also came from a local farming family, but hers was a rather grander family than her husband's.

John and Mary had eight children, two of whom died in childhood. William, their eldest son, was brought up with his parents and brothers and sisters in a house in Henley Street, Stratford. The house can still be seen today. There, in the same building, John Shakespeare worked and had his glover's shop.

The house in Stratford-upon-Avon where Shakespeare was born

Life in Stratford

Stratford-upon-Avon is in one of the loveliest parts of England. In Shakespeare's time it was a busy market town, filled with orchards and gardens. On market days the traders sold their goods in the streets and Will's father set up his stall alongside the other glove makers. Perhaps he took along his young son to help him.

Shakespeare's father began to take a leading part in Stratford life. Soon he became one of the most important men in the town. When Will was four years old, his father was made Bailiff of Stratford, which was an important and responsible job, similar to that of a mayor.

Going to school

A classroom scene in Shakespeare's time

Young Will was probably about seven years old when he became a pupil at Stratford Grammar School. There he would have been taught Latin. He would have learnt long Latin texts by heart and would also have studied the Bible, Latin literature and English history. In those days only boys went to school – girls stayed at home.

School began at 6.00 a.m. in summer, and at 7.00 a.m. in winter. No wonder Shakespeare, in one of his plays, describes 'the whining schoolboy, with his satchel . . . creeping like snail unwillingly to school'.

Shakespeare and the actors

At the time of Shakespeare's birth there were no theatres anywhere in England. Actors performed their plays in meeting halls, innyards, streets, or the homes of rich people. They travelled from town to town giving performances and many groups of actors visited Stratford. When Will's father was Bailiff he would greet them, and he probably had a front row seat in the Guildhall when they performed.

When Will was nine, the most famous acting company in England, called the Earl of Leicester's Men, came to Stratford. Their leading actor was James Burbage. (His son Richard later worked with Shakespeare for many years). Did nine-year-old Will watch their performance in Stratford? It is very likely that he did. Perhaps it was then that he first got a taste for the world of the theatre.

If so, it was a good time for a young man to become interested in drama. The first permanent theatres were just beginning to be built in the fields around London. Soon they were hugely successful: the great age of English drama was about to begin.

Marriage

Unfortunately, Will's father's fortunes began to take a turn for the worse. By the time Will was fourteen, his father was no longer as wealthy and successful as he had been.

This could have been the reason why the young man did not go on to university. Perhaps his education was halted so that he could help his father with his business.

The next thing we know is that Will married in November 1582, when he was eighteen. His bride, Anne Hathaway, was about seven years older than him. She was the daughter of a farmer in the

Anne Hathaway's cottage

nearby village of Shottery. By the time William was twenty-one, he and Anne had three children – a daughter called Susanna and then twins, a boy and a girl called Hamnet and Judith. They all lived at Henley Street with William's parents.

Leaving Stratford

No doubt it was hard for Will to make enough money to keep his growing family. This may be why he left Stratford at about this time. We know he left the town, but we do not know why, or where he went.

Some people say that he became a tutor. Others think he joined a troupe of actors. There is one story that says he got a job looking after horses outside London theatres; another that he had to leave Stratford because he had been poaching. Any of these stories could be true, but none of them can be proved.

Richard Burbage, Shakespeare's friend and fellow-actor

But we do know that Shakespeare somehow managed to get to London and there we next hear of him, some years later, as an actor and playwright.

A view of London in 1650

Success in London

London, towards the end of the sixteenth century, was an exciting place for anyone interested in drama. The new theatre buildings attracted huge audiences. There were many new playwrights. One of them, Christopher Marlowe, was the same age as Shakespeare and he wrote plays containing some of the finest and most dramatic poetry of the time. But, at the age of twenty-nine, Marlowe was killed in a brawl at an inn in London. Shakespeare's main rival was gone.

Marlowe was stabbed to death in an inn brawl

Marlowe, like most of the other new playwrights, was a 'university man'. He had studied at Cambridge. Shakespeare, of course, had not. Because he was not a 'university man', many fashionable people of his time looked down on him.

Shakespeare probably began his career acting in other people's plays and later started to write his own. By the time he was thirty he was well-known. An envious writer called Robert Greene wrote a sneering pamphlet about Shakespeare, calling him an 'upstart crow'. Perhaps he disliked him for being just an actor and not a 'university man'.

Shakespeare's name appears at this time amongst the members of the Lord Chamberlain's acting company. The Lord Chamberlain was an important officer of the Royal Household. He was responsible for all court entertainers and gave them his personal protection. His acting company was the best in England and a favourite with Queen Elizabeth I. Shakespeare wrote their plays and Richard Burbage was their star actor.

We know that Shakespeare was now doing well and making

An artist's impression of New Place, Shakespeare's house in Stratford

money because in 1597 he bought New Place, the second largest house in Stratford at that time. Shakespeare often returned to his family in Stratford. They must have been very proud of his success and delighted with their new home. Sadly, New Place no longer stands.

The Globe Theatre

The Bear Garden and Globe theatres, on the south bank of the Thames

Soon Shakespeare owned a share of the most famous of the Elizabethan theatres – the Globe. He wrote plays for the actors to perform there and he received part of the 'box office takings'.

The Globe stood on the south bank of the River Thames. It was circular and built of wood. The central area was largely open to the sky. Performances often took place in the afternoon so that the stage was lit by daylight. If it rained, there was no performance.

Inside, rows of galleries ran around the walls under a narrow thatched roof. The poorest people stood on the ground around the stage. Sometimes important visitors sat on the stage itself so as to get the best possible view. Altogether the Globe could hold an audience of about 2,500 people.

All kinds and classes of people (mostly men) attended Elizabethan theatres. The audiences behaved with much more freedom and were noisier than modern audiences. If we can imagine the atmosphere of a theatre, cinema, football pitch and boxing ring rolled into one, we can guess how exciting it was to go to the theatre in Shakespeare's time.

Londoners knew when a play would take place because they would see a flag flying from the theatre roof. This announced that a performance was about to begin.

The Globe's stage

The stage was a platform jutting out from one wall. Actors entered and exited through doors at the back of the stage. The galleries above were used as an 'upper' stage for special scenes. Here Juliet could appear on the 'balcony', with Romeo below, and Hamlet's father's ghost could walk along the 'castle walls'. Musicians played from galleries and upper windows, and in battle scenes, cannon would be fired from the windows.

Devils and ghosts could be summoned from 'hell' through a trap door in the stage floor. Gods and goddesses could be lowered from the stage roof – the 'heavens'.

In those days acting was not considered a respectable profession. Many people thought actors were little better than beggars and thieves. Women were not allowed to act and their parts were always played by boys.

Private performances

Not all performances took place at public theatres. Often the actors gave private entertainments for wealthy people in their homes. Shakespeare's later plays were also acted at the Blackfriars Theatre, which was roofed so they could be performed at night by candlelight. It was a more expensive and fashionable theatre than the Globe.

Sometimes the players acted at court in front of Queen Elizabeth herself. She especially liked fat Falstaff in *Henry IV*, and she asked Shakespeare to write another play about him. He obliged by writing *The Merry Wives of Windsor*.

When James I became King in 1603, he ordered that Shakespeare's company should be renamed 'The King's Men'. They often played at court and Shakespeare wrote *Macbeth* especially to please King James.

Shakespeare's plays

Shakespeare's plays still speak directly to audiences today. That is why his plays are performed constantly throughout the world. His comic characters make us laugh; his tragic figures make us feel very sad.

It is very difficult to give any real idea of what his plays are like, for they have to be seen to be enjoyed. But there are some important facts to know about them. Firstly, Shakespeare did not invent the plots of his plays. Instead, he used stories that were already quite well-known. Secondly, the plays are mostly written in poetry. Some of this is rhyming, but usually it is a special kind of non-rhyming poetry called blank verse.

Shakespeare wrote about thirty-seven plays altogether. Here we briefly mention a few of the best-known. A fuller list is given at the end of the book.

The comedies

Comedies, of course, are written to amuse and entertain. *A Midsummer Night's Dream* was probably written for a special performance at a court wedding. It has always been one of Shakespeare's most popular comedies.

In this play fairies, fine lords, ladies and rough country folk all gather together in a wood. Puck, a mischievous sprite, has gathered magic love juice from a flower, which, if pressed on to a sleeping person's eyes, will make them fall in love with the first person they see when they awaken.

Of course, everything goes wrong and soon the principal characters are falling in love with the wrong people. Titania, Queen of the Fairies, has the juice placed on her eyes and when she wakes she falls in love with Bottom – a poor weaver who is looking particularly foolish because he is wearing a donkey's head.

Eventually, all confusion is cleared up. Everything works out well and all the right people marry each other at the end of the play.

From the film of a famous Shakespeare comedy, The Taming of the Shrew

The tragedies

Shakespeare's four great tragedies, *Hamlet*, *Othello*, *King Lear* and *Macbeth* are some of the most powerful plays ever written.

The tragedies are serious and moving stories about great people who are overcome by unhappy events and finally destroyed. The scenes depict a world which is dark and violent, where love changes to hatred and good turns to evil.

A Japanese version of Macbeth – *a scene from the film* Throne of Blood

Macbeth is a play of foreboding and menace. The story is set in ancient Scotland during the reign of King Duncan. The words of the play describe wild and stormy scenes. Winds howl, ravens croak, bats flit around castle walls, and daggers drip with blood. On a wild heath live three witches. They have magic powers and can see into the future. These are some of their ingredients for a magic potion:

Eye of newt and toe of frog,
Wool of bat and tongue of dog,
Adder's fork and blindworm's sting,
Lizard's leg and howlet's wing . . .

When Macbeth meets the witches they tell him that one day he will be King of Scotland. He thinks continually about how he can become King and his wife, Lady Macbeth, encourages him to seize his chance. So, one night when King Duncan is a guest in his castle, Macbeth creeps into the King's room and murders him with a dagger.

Macbeth is then led into committing more terrible murders. He asks the witches' advice. Wrongly, he believes he is safe from punishment. But he is not, and he and Lady Macbeth finally meet their doom.

The histories

Many of Shakespeare's plays recreate famous historical events. Some tell of ancient Roman history, as in the plays *Julius Caesar*, *Antony and Cleopatra* and *Coriolanus*. Others tell the stories of legendary British rulers – *Cymbeline* and *King Lear* – and of later kings of England.

The first plays that Shakespeare wrote were *Henry VI* (which is three separate plays)

and *Richard III*. These tell the story of the Wars of the Roses, which were fought in England over a hundred years earlier. (The opposing sides in the wars used roses as their emblems; one side used a white rose and the other a red rose.)

In 1599 Shakespeare wrote *Henry V*. In this play he traced part of the story of the wars between England and France that

The wicked hunchback King plots with the Duke of Buckingham – from the film Richard III

had taken place two hundred years earlier. A particularly dramatic scene portrays the battle of Agincourt – which was a famous English victory. On the small stage of the Globe Theatre – 'this wooden O' as Shakespeare calls it in the play – were recreated the sounds of battle, the shouts of the soldiers and the clash of sword and armour. Cannon were fired from the windows above the stage to add to the excitement. No doubt the audience particularly enjoyed hearing King Henry's rousing battlecry as the fighting began: 'Cry God for Harry! England and Saint George!'

The poems

During Shakespeare's early years in London, between 1592 and 1594, the theatres were frequently closed because of the danger of plague spreading among the crowds. It was then that he began to write poetry for a young patron, the Earl of Southampton.

Shakespeare wrote elegant poems about love, in the style that the Elizabethans most enjoyed. His famous sonnets were a series of beautiful poems written for private reading among a small group of friends. The sonnets refer to a noble patron, a dark lady and a rival poet. Modern scholars do not agree about who these people were.

In his sonnets, Shakespeare is probably telling us more about his own feelings and thoughts than in any of his other writings, but we do not have the key to a full understanding of them.

Henry, Earl of Southampton, Shakespeare's patron and friend

A busy life

Shakespeare worked hard. He wrote about two plays a year. One of his most loved plays is *Romeo and Juliet* which he wrote in 1594. It tells the story of 'a pair of star-crossed lovers' in Verona in Italy, whose lives were blighted by a tragic feud between their families.

How else did Shakespeare spend his days? We know that he travelled continually to and from Stratford. In London he lived in lodgings, and in 1599 he was living in Southwark, near the Globe. Five years later he was lodging with a French wigmaker called Christopher Mountjoy, near St Paul's Cathedral.

King James I was crowned in 1604, and Shakespeare took part in the coronation procession through the streets of London.

Back home in Stratford, Shakespeare continued to buy property. He bought farmlands and houses, and his estate grew. He was now a wealthy and important citizen, entitled to be called 'gentleman', and his family was granted its own coat of arms.

Retirement to Stratford

In about 1613 Shakespeare retired to New Place, where he spent his time with his family. His son Hamnet had died when very young, but his two daughters, Susanna and Judith, were grown up and married.

In 1616 Shakespeare drew up his last will. He was probably already ill when he did this because his signature is in shaky handwriting. Most of his property went to his daughters. He left money to the poor people of Stratford. To his fellow actors Burbage, Heminges and Condell, he left money for them to buy 'memorial' rings – in memory of him. Many people have since wondered why he left only his 'second best bed' to his wife Anne.

A month later Shakespeare died at New Place, Stratford. He was buried on 25 April in the church where he had been baptized fifty-two years before. Later, a monument was set up in the church showing Shakespeare holding quill pen and paper.

Holy Trinity Church at Stratford-upon-Avon, where Shakespeare was baptized and where he is buried.

The First Folio

Seven years after his death, Shakespeare's fellow actors John Heminges and Henry Condell published a book containing thirty-six of his plays. Half of them had never been published before; the other half had been published only in inaccurate copies. So it is largely thanks to this book, called the First Folio, that Shakespeare's plays have been preserved.

A drawing of Shakespeare (right) appears at the beginning of the book. It was made some years after his death and may not be a good likeness of him.

Shakespeare's monument in Holy Trinity Church

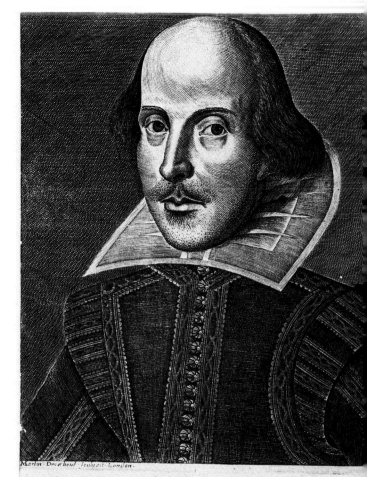

To the Reader.

This *Figure*, that thou here feeſt put,
It was for gentle *Shakeſpeare* cut
Wherein the *Graver* had a ſtrife
With *Nature*, to out-doe the *Life* :
O, could he but have drawn his *Wit*
As well in *Braſſe*, as he has hit
His *Face* ; the *Print* would then ſurpaſſe
All, that was ever writ in *Braſſe*.
But ſince he cannot, *Reader*, look
Not on his *Picture*, but his *Book*.

B. J.

The drawing and introductory verse which appeared in the First Folio

27

'So worthy a friend'

What did people who knew William Shakespeare think of him? Some obviously looked down on him because he was only a 'mere actor'. He was not high-born and he was not a 'university man', and actors, in general, were believed to be little better than rogues. His reputation was not as great then as it is today.

However, words from some of his contemporaries can tell us quite a lot about Shakespeare. One writer described him as 'honey-tongued', because he wrote such beautiful poetry. The same person also said that Shakespeare was one of the best English writers of comedy and tragedy.

Shakespeare's friends, the actors Heminges and Condell, wrote of him with great affection. They called him 'so worthy a friend and fellow' and described him as writing with 'ease and skill'. The poetry simply flowed from him, they said, so that 'we have scarce received from him a blot in his papers'.

Another famous playwright of the time, Ben Jonson, said of Shakespeare: 'I loved the man, and do honour his memory on this side of idolatry as much as any. He was indeed honest, and of an open and free nature.'

Ben Jonson, Elizabethan poet and dramatist, and friend of Shakespeare

Shakespeare's reputation

No book was written about Shakespeare until a hundred years after his death. Since then, thousands have been written. And of course his plays are performed and studied all over the world. He is now generally accepted to be one of the greatest writers who ever lived.

In Stratford many of the places associated with Shakespeare's family can still be visited. There, too, is the modern Royal Shakespeare Theatre, where the

The Royal Shakespeare Theatre at Stratford-upon-Avon

Statues of Falstaff and his creator stand in Bancroft Garden, Stratford

finest actors and actresses play the characters first created four hundred years ago. Although the figure of the playwright himself remains a little shadowy to us, his characters live on: Romeo and Juliet, Falstaff, Shylock, Bottom, Hamlet, Lady Macbeth and many, many more. As Ben Jonson wrote, Shakespeare 'was not of an age, but for all time'.

29

List of plays

This is the probable order in which Shakespeare's plays were written, with some of the known dates. Not all scholars agree on the order or the dates.

1591   Henry VI (Parts 1, 2 and 3)
Richard III
Titus Andronicus
Love's Labours Lost
The Two Gentlemen of
     Verona
The Comedy of Errors
The Taming of the Shrew

1594   Romeo and Juliet
A Midsummer Night's
     Dream
Richard II
King John
The Merchant of Venice

1597   Henry IV (Parts 1 and 2)
Much Ado About Nothing
Merry Wives of Windsor
As You Like It
Julius Caesar
Henry V
Troilus and Cressida

1601   Hamlet
Twelfth Night
Measure for Measure
All's Well That Ends Well
Othello

1606   King Lear
Macbeth
Timon of Athens
Antony and Cleopatra
Coriolanus

1609   Pericles

1611   Cymbeline
The Winter's Tale
The Tempest
Henry VIII

New words

Bailiff   An important town official, like a mayor or sheriff.

Blank verse   Verse that does not rhyme.

Comedy   A light and amusing kind of stage play.

Drama   A work that is performed by actors on a stage.

Folio   A large book made from sheets of paper folded in half.

Foreboding   A feeling that something bad will happen.

Legendary   Told as a legend – a story passed down from generation to generation.

Menace   Threat or danger.

Pamphlet   A short booklet.

Patron   A person who supports an artist by giving money.

Plague   A very infectious disease that used to sweep through countries, killing many people.

Playwright   A writer of plays.

Plot   The story told by a book, play or film etc.

Poaching   Illegally catching fish or game from someone else's land.

Sonnet   A special kind of poem with fourteen lines.

Tudor England   England during the reigns of the Tudor kings and queens, from 1457 to 1603.

Tragedy   A serious and moving kind of play, usually ending with the hero's death.

Books to read

Elizabeth I and Tudor England by Stephen White-Thomson (Wayland, 1984)

Shakespeare, Genius of the Theatre by Jacqueline Henrie (Chambers, 1980)

Shakespeare and his Theatre by John Russell Brown (Kestrel, 1982)

Shakespeare and the Players by C. Walter Hodges (Bell and Hyman, 1980)

William Shakespeare by Geoffrey Earle (Ladybird, 1981)

Picture credits

BBC Hulton Picture Library 4; British Tourist Authority 10 (upper); 26, 27 (lower), 29 (lower); Columbia Pictures/ National Film Archives 19; Connoisseur Films Ltd/National Film Archives 21; Crawford Films Ltd/National Film Archives 23; Michael Holford 10–11; Mansell Collection 24; National Portrait Gallery 28; National Portrait Gallery/ Wayland 4. Other pictures are from the Wayland Picture Library. Cover artwork by Richard Hook.

Index